ELMWOOD PARK PUBLIC LIBRARY
1 CONTI PARKWAY
ELMWOOD PARK, IL 60707
(708) 453-7645

1. A fine is charged for each day a book is kept
   beyond the due date. The Library Board may
   take legal action if books are not returned
   within three months

2. Books damaged beyond reasonable wear
   shall be paid for.

3. Each borrower is responsible for all books
   charged on this card and for all fines accruing
   on the same.

Power Rangers
OPERATION OVERDRIVE ™

ALL FIRED UP!

TM and © BVS Entertainment, Inc. and BVS International N.V. All rights reserved.
Adapted by Lynnor Vaughn

Dalmatian Press, LLC 2008. All rights reserved. Printed in the U.S.A.
The DALMATIAN PRESS name and logo are trademarks of Dalmatian Publishing Group, LLC, Franklin, Tennessee 37067.
No part of this book may be reproduced or copied in any form without written permission from the copyright owner.

07 08 09 10 BM 10 9 8 7 6 5 4 3 2 1
16436 Power Rangers 8x8 - Operation Overdrive: All Fired Up!

With the call of "Operation Overdrive," five skilled teens transform into the awesome Power Rangers.

Mack, the Red Ranger.
Dax, the Blue Ranger.
Rose, the Pink Ranger.
Ronny, the Yellow Ranger.
Will, the Black Ranger.

They are the only team in the world equipped to travel the globe to locate the five lost jewels of the Corona Aurora—before the forces of evil can find the jewels and use their powers against humanity.

Deep within the Inferno, a volcanic cave, the villainous Moltor—brother of the evil Flurious—was planning his next move.

"When I get the subatomic energy generator for my weather machine," he gloated, "I'll be more powerful than Flurious!"

He summoned his henchmen, the Lava Lizards, and they set out to steal the generator.

The Lava Lizards stopped an Energy Agency vehicle! With the driver held captive, they removed the subatomic energy generator.

Moltor smiled with glee. Little did he know that the Rangers had seen what he was up to.

"Let's Ranger up!" called Mack, the team's leader. "Operation Overdrive!"

The team arrived on the scene in their command ship—the Shark.

"We've gotta help the driver!" called Ronny, the Yellow Ranger.

"I'll save the driver," called Mack. "You guys go after Moltor!"

The Rangers battled the reptilian renegades as Moltor faced off with Mack.

With every fiery blast from Moltor, Mack sneered, "You're just makin' me mad!"

Suddenly, with a triumphant laugh, Moltor released the kidnapped driver—and sent him hurtling over a cliff!

Will, the Black Ranger, immediately went into action on his Hovertek Cycle. He zoomed over the cliff, rescuing the terrified driver in mid-air.

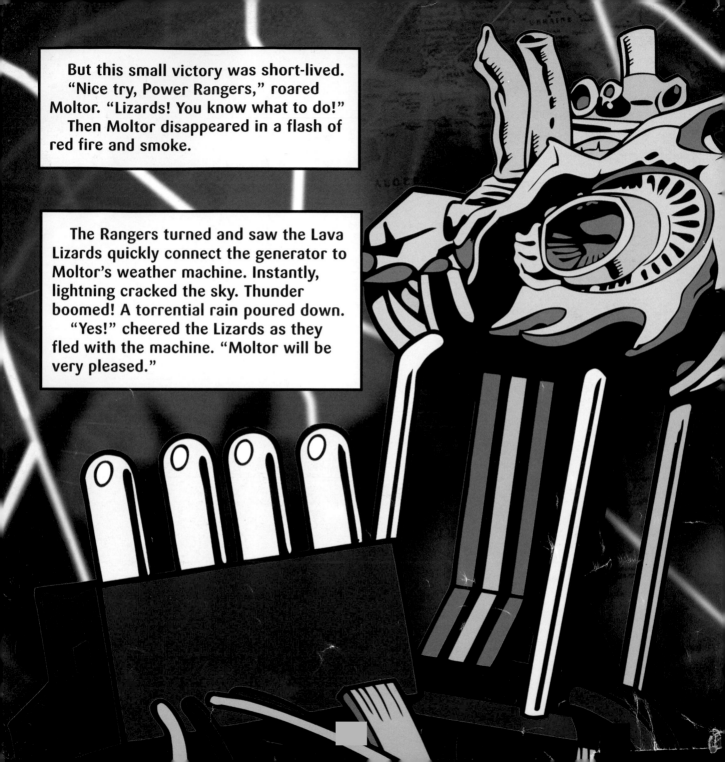

But this small victory was short-lived. "Nice try, Power Rangers," roared Moltor. "Lizards! You know what to do!" Then Moltor disappeared in a flash of red fire and smoke.

The Rangers turned and saw the Lava Lizards quickly connect the generator to Moltor's weather machine. Instantly, lightning cracked the sky. Thunder boomed! A torrential rain poured down. "Yes!" cheered the Lizards as they fled with the machine. "Moltor will be very pleased."

Moltor unleashed the power of his weather machine all around the world. The sun baked farmers' fields. Tornadoes ripped into cities. Hurricanes lashed beaches. Blizzards buried buildings in snow and ice. Floods swept houses away.

"The planet is in peril!" cried Dax, the Blue Ranger.

"We gotta stop Moltor and this wacky weather machine!" added Ronny.

"Okay, team—time to kick this battle into overdrive!" announced Mack. "Let's go find Moltor and his maniacal machine!"

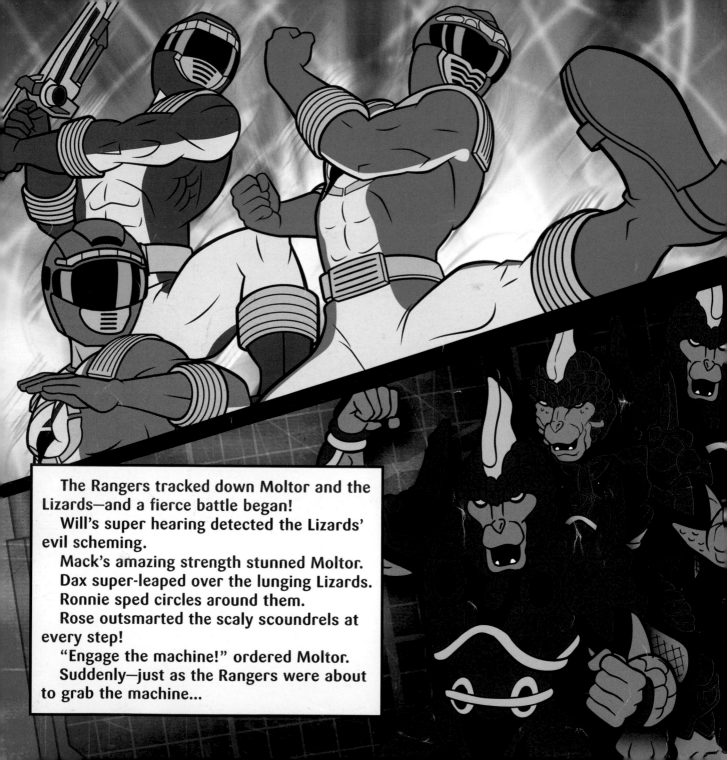

The Rangers tracked down Moltor and the Lizards—and a fierce battle began!

Will's super hearing detected the Lizards' evil scheming.

Mack's amazing strength stunned Moltor.

Dax super-leaped over the lunging Lizards.

Ronnie sped circles around them.

Rose outsmarted the scaly scoundrels at every step!

"Engage the machine!" ordered Moltor.

Suddenly—just as the Rangers were about to grab the machine...

...it took off into the air, spinning away on its own! As it spun, a flurry of blinding snow swirled around them.

"Wha—what's going on?" cried Moltor.

"The machine is doing it on its own!" cried Dax.

"You've lost control of your own evil device!" said Mack.

"I—I don't know what to do," blubbered Moltor.

"Let's get some extra power," said Mack. "Send in the Zords!"

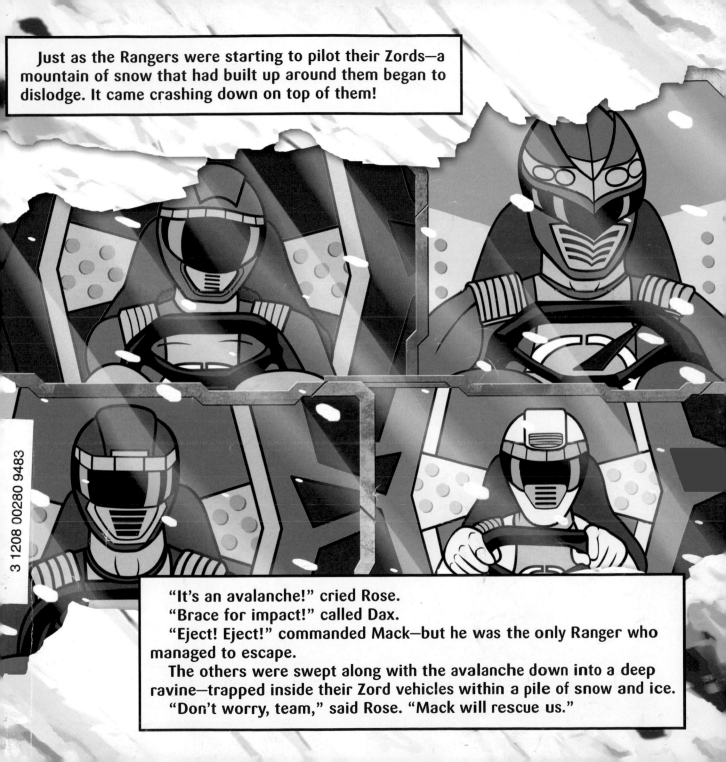

Just as the Rangers were starting to pilot their Zords—a mountain of snow that had built up around them began to dislodge. It came crashing down on top of them!

"It's an avalanche!" cried Rose.
"Brace for impact!" called Dax.
"Eject! Eject!" commanded Mack—but he was the only Ranger who managed to escape.
The others were swept along with the avalanche down into a deep ravine—trapped inside their Zord vehicles within a pile of snow and ice.
"Don't worry, team," said Rose. "Mack will rescue us."

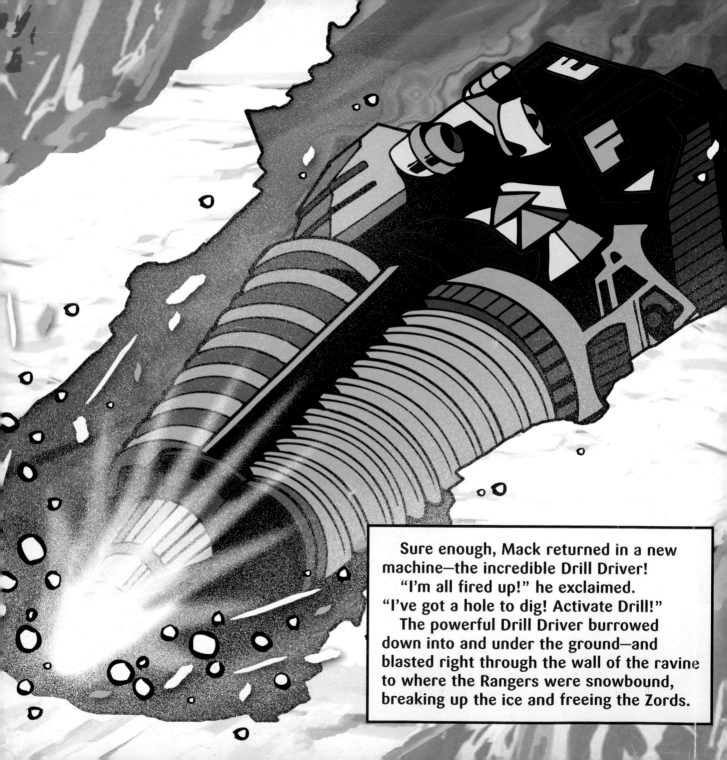

Sure enough, Mack returned in a new machine—the incredible Drill Driver!

"I'm all fired up!" he exclaimed. "I've got a hole to dig! Activate Drill!"

The powerful Drill Driver burrowed down into and under the ground—and blasted right through the wall of the ravine to where the Rangers were snowbound, breaking up the ice and freeing the Zords.

Having tracked the whirling machine, the team set their Zords in high gear. But as they roared upon the scene...

"Oh, no! There it is!" said Ronny. "And... and..."

"It's turning into a monster!" cried Will.

"Rangers, combine!" ordered the Red Ranger.

"You got it, Mack!" answered Will.

DRIVEMAX MEGAZORD! ACTIVATE! OPERATION OVERDRIVE!

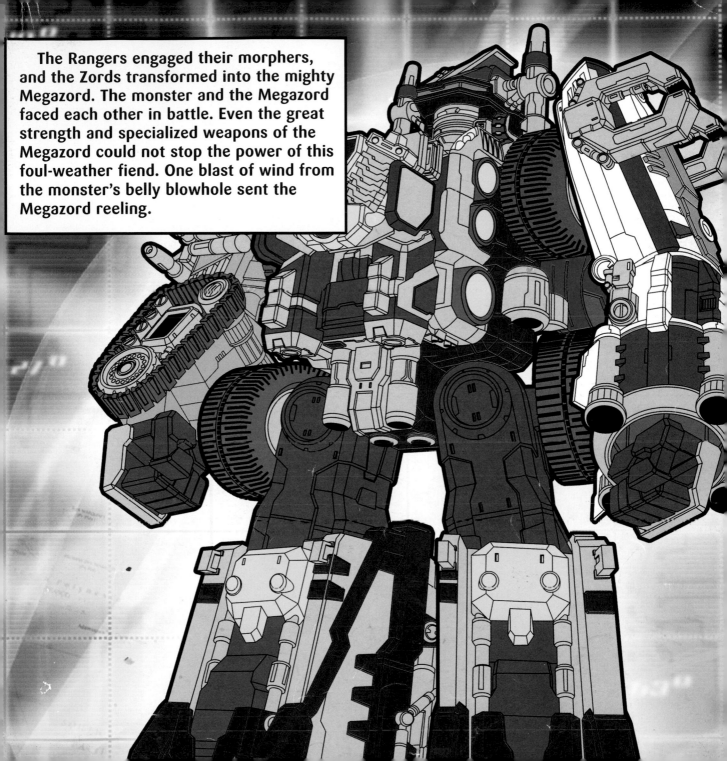

The Rangers engaged their morphers, and the Zords transformed into the mighty Megazord. The monster and the Megazord faced each other in battle. Even the great strength and specialized weapons of the Megazord could not stop the power of this foul-weather fiend. One blast of wind from the monster's belly blowhole sent the Megazord reeling.

"This monster is powerful," said Will.

"We can handle it!" urged Rose. "Come on, Rangers. We just need to use our smarts and come up with a plan."

"I've got an idea!" called Mack. "Let's see if we can combine the Megazord with the Drill Driver!"

"Great idea!" said Dax.

"Follow my lead!" said Mack. "Drivemax Megazord Drill Formation!"

"Awesome!" cried Ronny as the Drill Driver became the massive arm of the Megazord.

With a call of "Full power!" the Megazord drilled into the wind-blowing monster's middle—and ground it to pieces!

"All right! We did it!" cheered Rose.

"Now, that's what I call climate control!" chimed in Dax.

Back in his volcanic hideout, Moltor was sulking.
"Those meddling Rangers! I was so close! The power was mine—and I lost it!"
Moltor's brother Flurious appeared on his wall screen—mocking Moltor's defeat.

"Ha, ha, ha! I don't know 'weather' or not you've got what it takes to battle the Rangers—and find the jewels. You should just leave that to me."

"I'm a warrior!" fumed Moltor. "When I find the jewels to the Corona Aurora, I'll be the most powerful being in the universe—and you will kneel before me!"

"In your dreams, brother," said Flurious icily. "Only in your dreams."

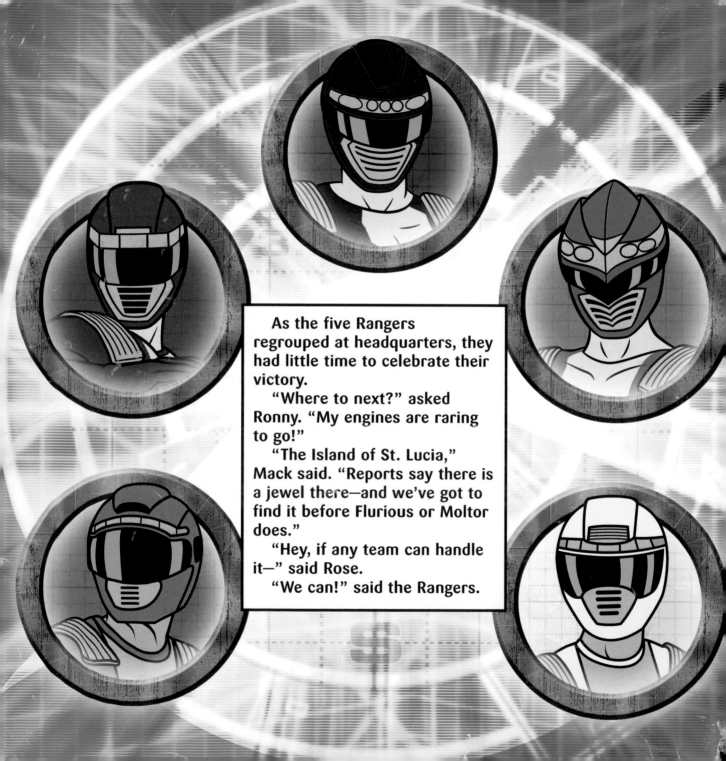

As the five Rangers regrouped at headquarters, they had little time to celebrate their victory.

"Where to next?" asked Ronny. "My engines are raring to go!"

"The Island of St. Lucia," Mack said. "Reports say there is a jewel there—and we've got to find it before Flurious or Moltor does."

"Hey, if any team can handle it—" said Rose.

"We can!" said the Rangers.